Athena Grace

The Adventures of Cody Wild by Athena Grace

ISBN 978-1-955136-97-6 (Paperback)

This book is written to provide information and motivation to readers. Its purpose is not to render any type of psychological, legal, or professional advice of any kind. The content is the sole opinion and expression of the author, and not necessarily that of the publisher.

Printed in the United States of America.
New Leaf Media, LLC
175 S. 3rd Street, Suite 200
Columbus, OH 43215
www.thenewleafmedia.com

Cody Wild

There was a little boy whose name was Cody Wild.
He likes to go exploring;
he's an adventurous child.

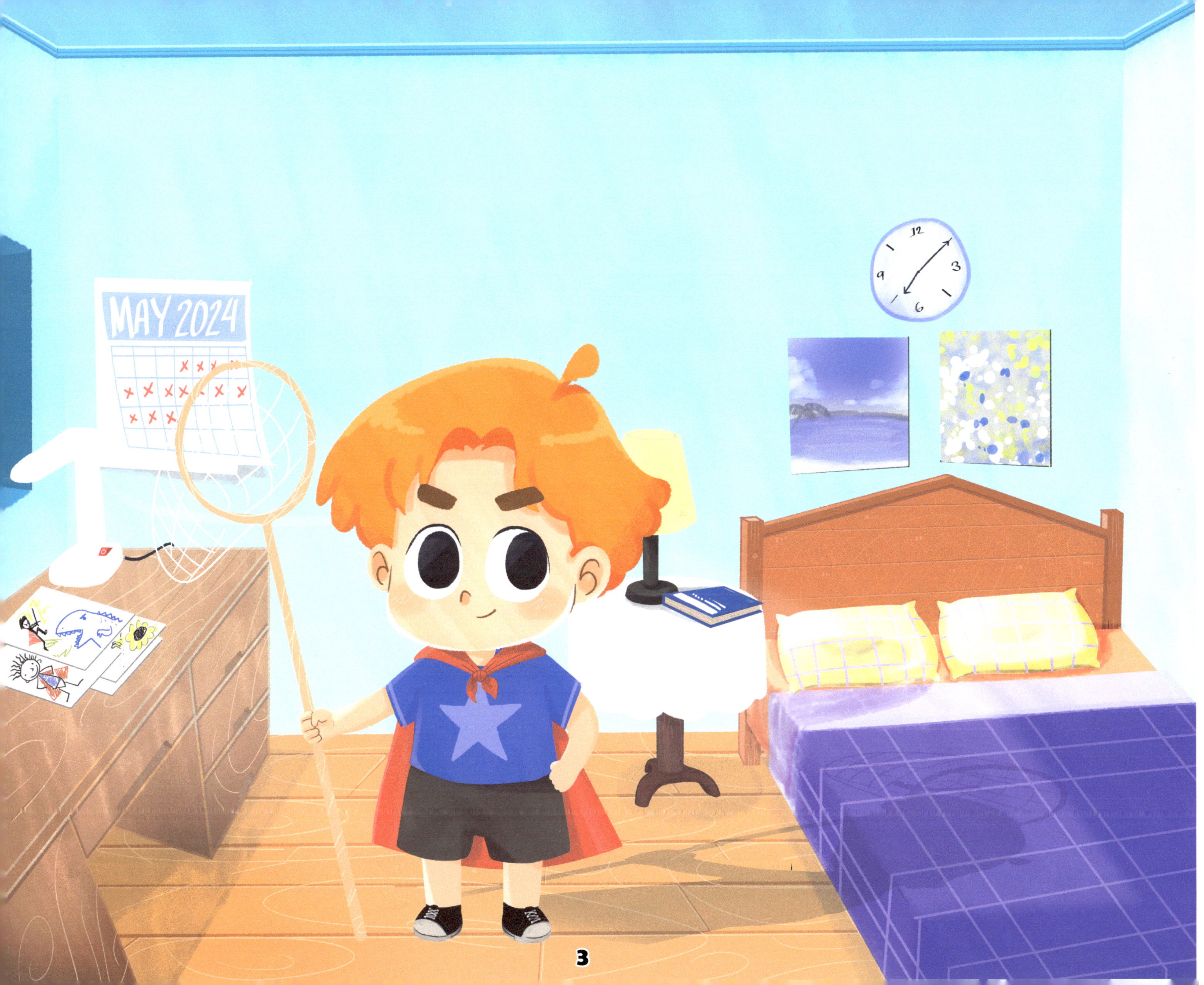
MAY 2024

So, what's a little boy to do when there's no one with which to play?
I know! I'll go outside, look around, and greet the day!

Look there in the grass. What do I see? It's green and it hops up and down.

It even has two large antennae and long legs. Listen, what is that sound?

So, can you guess what is it?
What did I see?
A dog, a cat, a bat, or a bee?

Well, a dog isn't green, nor does he jump up and down.
A dog barks and runs with his dog friends.
Then, he digs in the ground.
So, if it's not a dog.
Could it be a furry cat?
But, have you even seen a cat that is green-- think about that!

Cats like to purr, cuddle, and have fun all day. They like to chase mice--they're just that way.

So, If it isn't a cat,
perhaps Cody saw a bat?
No, gee whiz, wow!
Just think about that!

A bat hangs upside down,
and has a big wings to fly. But, you only see
him at night as he flies through the sky.

Well, If it isn't a dog, a cat, or a bat.
Let's think... let's see.
The only thing left is a little bumble bee.
But can green be the color of a
little bumblebee?
Think about that, think hard...
Let's see.

No, I think bees are yellow and black,
and fly very fast.
Now by thinking it through,
I bet you have an answer at last.

So, do you know what it is?
Can you guess like me.

You did it!
You know the answer--it's a green
grasshopper... see?

The Adventures Of Cody Wild

There was a little boy whose name was Cody Wild.
He likes to go exploring; he's an adventurous child.

So, what's a little boy to do when there's no one with which to play?
I know! I'll go outside, look around, and greet the day!

Look there in the grass. What do I see? I'ts green and it hops up and down.
It even has two large antennae and long legs. Listen, what is that sound?

So, can you guess what it is? What did I see?
Was it a dog, a cat, a bat, or a bee?

Well, a dog isn't green, nor does he jump up and down.
A dog barks and runs with his dog friends. Then, he digs in the ground.

So, if it's not a dog. Could it be a furry cat?
But, have you ever seen a cat that is green-- think about that!

Cats like to purr, cuddle, and have fun all day.
They like to chase mice-- they're just that way.

So, if it isn't a cat, perhaps Cody saw a bat?
No, gee whiz, wow! Just think about that!

A bat hangs upside down, and has big wings to fly.
But, you only see him at night as he flies through the sky.

Well, if it isn't a dog, a cat, or a bat. Let's think... let's see.
The only thing left is a little bumblebee.

But can green be the color of a little bumblebee?
Think about that, think hard... Let's see.

No, I think bees are yellow and black, and fly very fast.
Now by thinking it through, I bet you have an answer at last.

So, do you know what it is? Can you guess like me.
You did it! You know the answer-- it's a green grasshopper... see?

Printed in the USA
CPSIA information can be obtained
at www.ICGtesting.com
CBHW042304230724

12037CB00004B/48